To Alita

Follow

Ramsey (David Peterson)

With love from Gigi!

RAMSEY
The Pink Rhinoceros

DAVID ASHLEY PETERSON

ILLUSTRATIONS BY MARY EARLE

 FriesenPress

Suite 300 - 990 Fort St
Victoria, BC, V8V 3K2
Canada

www.friesenpress.com

David is an ordained minister in the Anglican Church and a teacher. He has taught in both elementary and high school. He is happy to bring to you Ramsey – a story that has been in his imagination for over thirty years. David enjoys photography, guitar and spending time with Tillie the Wonder Dog – and writing of course!

ISBN
978-1-5255-8806-8 (Hardcover)
978-1-5255-8805-1 (Paperback)
978-1-5255-8807-5 (eBook)

1. Juvenile Fiction, Animals, Hippos & Rhinos

Distributed to the trade by The Ingram Book Company

To my beloved Mother,
who helped create **Ramsey**,

and to my sweet Milagros,
who encouraged me to write this book.

Many thanks to Mary Earle, illustrator.

RAMSEY was a **rhinoceros**.

Ramsey was a **PINK** rhinoceros.

Being **pink** was odd for a rhino, but it was even stranger for a boy rhinoceros.

People used to stare when **Ramsey** and his mother went shopping.

Though they did not mean to be unkind, he could hear them whispering to their friends, "Did you see that young, **pink** rhinoceros? How odd he looks."

At school, while Professor Perigrinus Pelican wrote on the blackboard, the other students would stare at **Ramsey**. This made **Ramsey** blush, and that made this **pink** rhinoceros even **pinker**!

Ramsey also stood out from his classmates in another way. You see, at **Ramsey's** school, all the kids enjoyed clubs or other after-school activities.

The Chess Club had very smart students like Oswald Owl. The Rugby Team had very strong animals, such as

Barnabas Bear. The Cheerleaders had beautiful birds like Petunia Peacock. The Choir had many lovely songbirds like Neanie Nightingale. To his surprise, **Ramsey** saw that even Charlie Crow was in the Choir, and while his singing voice was not *so* good, he bravely tried his best.

But **Ramsey** didn't join any of the activities...he just watched the others play at their clubs or on their sports teams. One afternoon, he decided to watch the soccer practice on the field. He felt sad because he liked soccer, but he was afraid to join the team. He watched one small bunny trying to kick the ball into the net, but all his shots missed. He became frustrated after many tries.

"Why bother?" he wailed to Mr. Bear, the coach.

Coach Bear looked thoughtful and then said, "I think you'll get there. Keep trying, and just remember," he said with a twinkle in his eye, "you miss every goal you don't shoot for."

Ramsey thought about that all the way home.

When the school day was done, **Ramsey** would go to his room. **Ramsey's** room also happened to be **pink**. His bedspread was **pink**. His walls were **pink**—even his desk was **pink**.

Ramsey loved **pink**, but even more than that, he loved to listen to his (**pink**) CD player.

From the day he was a little **pink** bundle of rhino in his **pink** crib, **Ramsey** loved music.

As soon as the first strains of Tchaikovsky or Mozart began to play, he started to dance. He danced around his room until his mother came in to put him into bed.

One day, as **Ramsey** and his mom were shopping, he saw a notice board with hundreds of posters that said:

The Pan-Animal Theatre Company

— is —

Proud to Present

the Popular Performer

**THEODORE
TWINKLE TOES TIGER**

Dancing with the Royal Animal Ballet
— May 6th 8pm. —

Ramsey's heart leapt! His eyes shone! How he would love to go! While his mother was paying for the groceries, Ramsey took a poster, folded it up carefully, and tucked it into the pink pocket of his pink raincoat.

Later that night, at the Rhino Home, while his mother and father were sipping coffee and reading the daily newspaper, *Who's Who in the Zoo*, Ramsey came into the room. He stood before them and nervously cleared his throat.

"Ahem."

Two pairs of rhino eyes peered over their newspapers.

"Hello, Ramsey," said his father. "Are you having trouble with your homework?"

"No, thank you," Ramsey returned politely.

"Do you have a tummy ache, Dear?" asked his mother.

"No, I'm fine."

"What would you like, Dear?" asked his mother.

Ramsey handed the poster to her.

She read it and her eyebrows went up, then she looked down her horn at him.

"Oh, **Ramsey**! Surely you don't want to go to that!"

Ramsey looked crestfallen.

"Let us see," said **Ramsey's** father, putting on his spectacles and taking the paper. He took out his pipe and filled the bowl with his favourite tobacco, *Safari Sunset*. He lit it and puffed away thoughtfully until the air was quite blue.

He looked long and hard at his son, then smiled a strange smile.

"Alright, **Ramsey**, I'll take you."

Mother, not to be left out, declared "Well, I'm going too!"

Ramsey hugged his parents. He was so happy he danced an extra hour in his room.

As **Ramsey** was drifting off to sleep, he heard his parents talking in the next room.

"Why didn't you want **Ramsey** to go to the ballet?" Father asked gently, "I think he wants to be a dancer." There was a long silence.

"I guess because it doesn't seem right for a boy to do that," Mother replied. Then, after a moment, she said in an embarrassed voice, "I don't really know why... I can't explain it."

After a short silence, Father said thoughtfully, "When I was in school, I wanted to learn cooking, but my father wouldn't let me. He said that was what girls did."

"Hmm...my parents wouldn't let me learn how to fix cars," Mother said sadly. "I always wanted to."

"Perhaps," said father, "we should let **Ramsey** try what he wants to do." **Ramsey** couldn't hear much more and drifted off to sleep, feeling that Things would be alright after all.

In the morning, there were three tickets on the breakfast table...

At last came the day of the performance. They traveled two hours by car to Ottawa. They had front row seats. The beautiful theatre was packed; many had come specially to see Theodore Twinkle Toes Tiger. Twinkle Toes was performing with the beautiful and talented ballerina, Lynda Lemur. **Ramsey** read that Twinkle would swoop Lynda high in the air as they danced.

About twenty minutes to curtain, **Ramsey** excused himself to go to the bathroom. Near the "Gentlemen Animals' Bathroom," he saw a partly open door that seemed to lead backstage.

He allowed himself a peek… and what he saw was wonderful. Backstage was a magical world of theater!

There were sets of painted buildings with doors to go through and windows that opened and shut.

There were piles of props for the show: crowns that glittered, swords in scabbards, helmets topped with feathers, and trumpets to blow—everything you could think of was there!

He was entranced. He walked further and further in. Animals dressed in black clothing scurried about, setting up the stage.

Behind a closed door, he heard a growly voice yell, "What do you mean Twinkle Toes is sick? He *can't* be! Not five minutes to curtain! It's a disaster! He's the only one who can lift Lynda!"

A door opened and a very cross-looking lion stepped out. He wore big sunglasses, a French beret, and a stripy blue and white shirt. He slammed the door with his tail and buried his head in his paws. He was so upset he threw his script on the stage and jumped up and down on it a few times.

Ramsey nervously took a step backwards and knocked over a stage light, which fell with a crash.

The lion looked up. He gazed at **Ramsey** intently.

"You there! Yes, you! Can you dance?"

Ramsey stood still as stone, then, to his surprise, he nodded his head.

The lion gave a toothy grin. "Wonderful! You're hired, son! I'm Leopold, director of the show. Come with me...er..."

"**Ramsey**!" the **pink** rhino squeaked.

"Fine name, fine name," growled the lion as he grabbed him by the shoulder and escorted him to a changing room.

Before **Ramsey** knew it, several monkeys were scampering around, fixing up his costume.

They placed **pink** ballet slippers on his feet. They fixed a frilly **pink** ruff around his neck. But there was a problem. There wasn't a pair of tights big enough for **Ramsey**.

Through the curtain, Leopold could hear the crowd getting restless! He was already five minutes late! Something had to be done.

Leopold spied a long, **pink** curtain hanging backstage. He gave it a tremendous yank and pulled it down. He gave it to the two monkeys, who wound it around and around and around **Ramsey's** middle and then fastened it with a **pink** diaper pin. Two peacocks powdered makeup onto **Ramsey** and his horn, then led him to Leopold.

Leopold quickly introduced **Ramsey** to Lynda Lemur, the star ballerina.

The crowd began to murmur and cough impatiently. There was no time left.

"Just *dance!*" he said to **Ramsey** as he slipped through the curtain to introduce the show. The house hushed instantly.

"Ladies, Gentlemen, Boys and Girls, Beasts and Animals, Welcome to the Royal Animal Ballet!"

There was a thunderous crash of applause.

Ramsey thought he heard a voice, which sounded a lot like his mother's say, "Where on earth is **Ramsey**? He'll be late!"

"It is with deep regret," Leopold continued, "that Theodore Twinkle Toes Tiger cannot be with us tonight due to illness, but—"

His voice was drowned out by a massive groan of disappointment and a murmur that grew to the sound of a hive of angry bees.

"But," he said again, "at *very* short notice and at no additional expense to you, we present the debut of **Ramsey**, the **Pink** Rhinoceros."

There was a half-hearted applause. Over the clapping, **Ramsey** distinctly heard his mother say "**Ramsey**? Surely not *our* **Ramsey**!"

The orchestra swelled. Floodlights shone and the curtain parted and there, in the spotlight, stood one very **pink** rhinoceros.

For a moment, he stood blinking against the lights— transfixed by the hundreds of eyes gazing at him.

The music rose and began its melody... but something was *wrong*! **Ramsey** couldn't move a muscle! He had never danced in public before, and he was frozen like a statue with stage fright!

The eyes stared at him coldly and expectantly, and **Ramsey** stared back wide-eyed. Suddenly, he wasn't thinking about being on stage. For some reason, he was thinking about the brave little bunny who tried to play soccer. In his mind, he heard the coach's words:

"Remember, you miss every goal you don't shoot for."

Suddenly, he saw kind eyes, helpful eyes—the eyes of his father, and they were proud eyes. His father winked, and something like joy burst in **Ramsey's** heart. This was *his moment*, his dream. His goal was to be a dancer, and he would *shoot*.

He began to sway in time with the music. He waved one leg and then another. He trotted gracefully around the stage. He tiptoed terrifically. He leapt luxuriously. His polished horn flashed in the spotlight.

Applause sounded in his ears. Lynda Lemur joined him in a graceful duet, and he effortlessly lifted her up by one hoof. He tossed her into the air, twirling like a top, and caught her like a feather. They jived. They tangoed. They discoed and boogied. They pirouetted the evening away.

Finally, the music crescendoed as the ballet ended with a flourish, and as all the animals came on stage, they joined paws and hooves and bowed. The audience was on their feet cheering. Mother was clapping the hardest, and Father had tears of joy in his eyes. Cries of "encore!" and "bravo!" filled the theatre. Roses were thrown onto the stage. Leopold presented Lynda and **Ramsey** with big bouquets and with a special envelope for **Ramsey**.

The Rhino family was tired but excited as they drove home.

"You know," said Mother thoughtfully, "I think I'll take a night school course in mechanics."

"Good idea," said Father. "I think I'll take up cooking".

Ramsey was sleepy and didn't understand, but somehow, he felt happy for his parents.

When **Ramsey** finally got to bed, on his dresser was a $1,000.00 cheque towards dancing lessons, a "Thank You" card from Theodore Twinkle Toes Tiger, and a glossy black and white photograph of Lynda Lemur.

"To **Ramsey** with love," it said with a dozen Xs for kisses. He could not wait to show it to his friends at school the next day.

Ramsey smiled as he shut his eyes, dancing into his dreams and into his future.

CPSIA information can be obtained
at www.ICGtesting.com
Printed in the USA
BVHW020727290922
648157BV00002B/26

9 781525 588068